VIOLENT EN

PARANORMAL

A collection of ghost stories from North West Indiana

By

Lara G. Vargas

DEDICATION

This book is dedicated to my parents, to my siblings and their families and to my wife and our children. Writing this book took time away from them and I appreciate their understanding and support.

EPIGRAPH

Pray first, then the rest is easy.

>   Lara G.
>   Vargas

FOREWORD

Professor Lara Gonzales Vargas was born in East Chicago Harbor, Indiana and lived in Gary for twenty years before joining the Army and moving away from the region. Although a strong believer in the paranormal, Professor Vargas' forty years of experience in law enforcement, accident investigation and military intelligence has made him very slow to believe much of what he sees on television.

In some of his college courses Professor Vargas teaches his students the three basic elements to conducting a thorough investigation: observation, interviews and reviewing existing evidence and documentation.

As much as was possible, he applied these basic elements of investigation against the stories in this book. In the end, he could neither prove nor disprove any of the claims made by the people who shared these stories.

INTRODUCTION

If hauntings are the result of violent deaths, Northwest Indiana should be one of the most haunted places in America; that is of course, if you believe the endless number of self-proclaimed paranormal "experts" who seem to be on one ridiculous television show or another nearly every day of the week.

Scientists, journalists, and even the clergy have investigated claims of the paranormal, sometimes for years without ever experiencing a single thing that could be considered "paranormal." Yet nearly every one of those ghost hunting shows claims to catch something paranormal on every episode. And if you haven't noticed, nearly every show has a self-proclaimed "Medium" on the team who claims the ability to communicate with the dead.

Don't get me wrong, I'm a true believer in the paranormal, and I even enjoy watching some of those shows. I actually make a game out of predicting how long it will be before some disembodied spirit demands that they, "Get out!" And if you haven't noticed, it happens on nearly every show. And there is always someone getting scratched or pushed by an unseen hand.

I also like to watch those shows to catch up on all the new paranormal investigative tools like the "Spirit Box," whatever that is; the EVPs recorder, and of course the EMF reader. All of which are "must have" tools in any real ghost hunter's tool box.

I make fun of Hollywood a lot, but I have to admit that some of those television shows and some movies have been very educational. I don't have any real numbers, but I'll bet that at least 90 percent of everything we know about the paranormal we learned from Hollywood. For example, from cult classic, *Night of The Living Dead*, we first learned that you must shoot a zombie in the head to destroy it. And from the movie, *Poltergeist* we learned that messing around "ancient Indian burial grounds," causes all kinds of paranormal things to occur. And before the blockbuster hit, *The Amityville Horror,* no one had never heard an evil spirit utter the words, "Get Out!"

I believe that disturbing cemeteries is a bad thing, but nobody has yet been able to tell me exactly why disturbing an ancient Indian burial ground is worse than disturbing a Greek Orthodox cemetery. But if it really is that bad, we're in big trouble, because nearly all of our major cities are built directly on top of where the Indians once lived and where they buried their dead. Maybe that's why cities like Chicago, Detroit and Gary, Indiana, are so full of violence and therefore so full of paranormal activity.

The South has its Civil War battlefields and slave plantations, all of which were the sites of unimaginable suffering, cruelty and deaths, and Northwest Indiana has countless building, alleys, homes and streets where unimaginable bad things have occurred; and still does.

I absolutely do believe in ghost and I also believe that people can get demonically possessed, I've seen it firsthand. I've never seen a young girl spin her head around but I have seen real evil in the eyes of a twelve-year-old boy who once demanded that an older man who was holding a gun to my temple, pull the trigger.

I also believe that hauntings are the residual effects of real bad things that happened at a location. I think that if an event is traumatic or emotional enough, that the energy expelled will replay itself visually or audibly from time to time if the atmosphere and conditions are just right.

I'm a trained investigator, a retired military officer, and a college professor, none of which qualifies me as an expert in the paranormal, but it has made me very slow to believe things just because I saw it on a television show or read about it on the Internet. And just for the record, I do believe that some people have physic abilities; but I've never met one and I doubt that very many of the ones who claim to be actually are.

PREFACE

Just like anyone else, I grew up hearing family members, friends and neighbors tell ghost stories that they all swore were true. But it wasn't until the incident involving the supposed "Demon House," in the Glen Park neighborhood of Gary, Indiana where I grew up, did the idea ever occur to me to write down some of those stories as a collection of North West Indiana hauntings.

Not all violent endings that occur in NW Indiana were crime related. With the steel mills, railroads and waterways that the region is built around, many violent endings are the result of accidents. Accidents, but none the less violent endings.

PROLOGUE

There are many cities and towns that make up the NW Indiana region. For the purpose of this book, I concentrated my focus on paranormal events that supposedly occurred in the cities of Gary, Hammond, Merrillville and East Chicago.

The stories in this book are other people's experiences, and not necessarily mine. Although I collected over 100 stories in preparation for writing this book, I used only the ones that passed my four points check list:
1) I only accepted first-hand accounts; 2) I only accepted stories that occurred in the region; 3) I physically visited each location where the events supposedly occurred; and 4) All elements of the story had to be consistent. In other words, if the story changed during multiple telling's and re-telling's, I didn't use it.

Table of Content

Chapter One - A portal to hell in Gary, Indiana?

Chapter Two - The Menendez's demonically possessed house.

Chapter Three - Richie's haunted house.

Chapter Four - The Party Line.

Chapter Five - A phantom train?

Chapter Six - The dead lady outside of Lew Wallace High School.

Chapter Seven – Next time call a freaking tow truck!

Chapter Eight - Ray's big spooky house.

Chapter Nine - My murdered ex-girlfriend.

Chapter Ten - Night of the walking dead chick.

Chapter Eleven - The witch in our back yard.

Conclusion

Chapter One

A portal to hell in Gary, Indiana

In 2012 a woman in Gary, Indiana claimed that she had seen her daughter levitate above her bed and that her son was possessed by evil spirits. What made this story particularly interesting to me were the number of professional people who backed up the lady's claims.

According to what I read about the case, employees with Gary's Youth and Family Services, hospital staff, the clergy and even a high-ranking member of the Gary Police Department all claimed to have experienced things that made them believe that the woman's claims were true. In one instance a social worker and some hospital staff, reported seeing the woman's little boy walk backwards up a wall.

The story was so sensational that it caught the attention of Mr. Zak Bagans, the host of the popular television show "Ghost Adventures," who purchased the house sight unseen and after investigating it, had it demolished. According to Mr. Bagans, in the basement of that house, he and his investigators found a "portal to hell."

When I read the story, I couldn't help but laugh, not because I didn't believe the woman or Mr. Bagans, I actually did believe them. I just found it very funny that such a big deal was being made over one house. Obviously, Mr. Bagans didn't know the history of Gary, Indiana, or as one comic described it, "the only city in America where you can drive five miles in any direction and never leave the scene of the crime."

Reading about this case and watching the documentary styled film "Demon House," made me think of some other scary stories I heard from people when I lived in Gary. After sharing some of those stories with my wife and kids, they encouraged me to write them down as a collection of NW Indiana ghost stories. This book is exactly that, a collection of creepy and supposedly true paranormal events that happened to people in Northwest Indiana.

I grew up hearing a lot of these so-called ghost stories, but for the sake of getting this book written, I focused on just a handful.

I don't know if what these people told me is true. I do know, that they've been telling the same stories the same way for as long as I can remember which is significant, because as a trained investigator, I've learned that people have little trouble remembering things that actually happened or that they believe happened. No matter how many times you ask them or how you ask them, they will tell the story the same way each time, frontwards or backwards, and their story never change.

I've changed the names of the people who contributed these stories to protect them from any undue attention. I've also omitted any actual addresses to prevent anyone from trying to explore the places mentioned in this book and getting themselves killed.

Chapter Two

The Menendez's demonically possessed house

The Individual telling this story is Eric. Eric is a retired U.S Steel employee who claims that between the years of 1964 and 1968, in Gary's Emerson neighborhood, friends of his family lived in a demonically possessed house.

Somewhere off of 19th Avenue on the west side of Gary, there's a house that once belonged to friends of my family and I remember vividly that the only time we ever went to that house was when one of the eight kids had a birthday party and parties were always during the day, always during the summer, and were always held outside in their back yard. If the weather ever got bad, the party was never moved inside, it was just over.

I also remember that anytime a guest had to use the bathroom, one of the older kids or one of the parents would escort their guest into the house and wait in the house to escort them back out.

One time the mother and father nearly lost their minds because one of the younger kids left a guest in the house alone. While the mother was chewing the boy out in-front of the entire party, the father ran as fast as he could into the house and after a minute or two walked out with the woman who the kid had left in the house. Being a kid at the time, I simply believed that they didn't trust anyone in their house, but later I learned that they were afraid of what the house might do to anyone who was left alone in their house.

One night, one of the older girls spent the night at our house and scared the crap out of all of us when she told us about the things that went on in her house. For example, she told us that several times since they lived there, their dresser drawers would be infested with maggots and worms and then completely disappear leaving no signs of ever being there.

She also told us about the night that she and her siblings were sitting on their window seat, watching the snow fall against the street lights while they waited for their father to come home from working the 4 PM to 12 AM shift at the mill. She said they watched as their father parked his car in the drive-way and carefully walked up their long slippery sidewalk towards their front door. She claimed that out of nowhere, a man appeared behind her father and began to follow him towards the house. She described the man as Caucasian, very tall, skinny and wearing a tuxedo and a tall shiny black hat like the one Abraham Lincoln wore. She described how her father smiled at them when he saw them at the window but when he saw the terrified looks on their faces, he turned around and saw the man walking up behind him and began to run for the front door. She described how her mother held the front door open for him while frantically screaming for him to run. She said that her father practically dove into the house just as her mother slammed the door shut behind him. She said that the man made no attempts to force his way into the house, "He just stopped, turned around and walked off," she said.

If that that doesn't make the hair on the back of your neck stand on end, there was another time when the mother showed up at our house with the five youngest kids in tow, so hysterical that we thought she had lost her mind. When she finally calmed down enough to talk, she told us that she and the kids where in bed when she decided to go downstairs to make sure that the front porch light was on for her husband who would be getting home after midnight. She claimed that right in the middle of their living room, was a large white horse, "just lying there." Each of kids claimed that when they heard their mother scream, they all came running and saw the horse too. They also described how they had to walk sideways past the horse to get out of the house.

I remember that the woman was very worried that her husband would be home soon and worry when he didn't find them there. I also remember thinking to myself that I would be more worried about him walking into the house with that horse in the living room.

Because it was a Friday night, my oldest brother was out with his friends, so my father drove over to their house by himself and waited outside until their father and older kids got home. Together the five of them checked out the house and found nothing out of the ordinary. Regardless, that night their entire family stayed at our house until the sun came up.

Chapter Three

Richie's haunted house

The Individual telling me this story is Richie. Richie is a retired Air Force Intelligence Officer, who claims to have experienced the following between the years 1974 and 1981, when he lived in Gary's West Glen Park neighborhood.

In 1974 we moved out of the predominately Black and Mexican neighborhood of Brunswick and into the all-white, upper middle-class neighborhood of West Glen Park.

The brick bungalow styled house came up for sale after the elderly couple who lived there for about 40 years, died. The woman died of natural causes but her husband of over 50 years blew his brains out in the main floor bathroom shortly after laying his wife to rest at nearby Oak Hill Cemetery.

To me the house was absolutely beautiful. The main floor has two large bedrooms, an eat-in kitchen, a formal dining room, a big living room, a pantry, and a wooden ironing board in the kitchen that folded into the wall. The house also has 14-foot-high ceilings, crown molding and large base boards in every room. And in the main floor bathroom where the previous owner took his own life, there is porcelain bath tub big enough for three people to sit in comfortably.

But what made the house so great from the very moment I laid eyes on it was the basement. Nearly all Midwestern homes have basements, but this basement was finished and subdivided into two separate apartments. Each side complete with a bedroom, a living room, an eat-in kitchen, a bathroom and its own separate staircase to the main floor. The side of the basement I claimed as my teenage bachelor pad had an "L" shaped staircase that led into the kitchen and my brother's side had a spiral staircase that led into the living room. Both sides were separated by a heavy wooden door that locked from both sides, and for some unknown reason, on my side, there was an old fashioned door bell, the kind you have to twist to make the bell ring.

The paranormal stuff, for lack of a better term, started almost immediately after we moved into the house. At first, we didn't consider it paranormal or supernatural, just weird.

Within a week of living there, my brother Luis began having dreams of an old man who would walk around the house as if he were looking for something. And then my youngest sister Lisa began having a dream in which an old man would lean into the bedroom she shared with our older sister Ester, turn on the light and stare at them for a few seconds before turning off the light and walking away.

And then Ester also began to have a dream of an old man who would walk into their bedroom, turn on the lights, and stare at her and Lisa before turning off the lights and walking away. Weird yes, but not paranormal.

One morning at the breakfast table, Luis, Lisa, and Ester began comparing notes, and it did appear that they were describing the same old man. Was that supernatural? I didn't think so at the time, neither did our mom. We came to feel that they were making each other believe that they were dreaming about the same old man.

And then very early one Saturday morning our entire family, minus my father who had not yet returned home from working the overnight shift at Inland Steel, were awakened by the sound of my brother Luis screaming hysterically.

It was about seven o'clock in the morning and the sound of Luis screaming bloody murder nearly sent me through the ceiling. I immediately jumped out of bed and ran to the door that separated my side of the basement from his and found that it was locked from his side. I ran up the stairs into our kitchen and was shocked to find my brother, both of my sisters and our mother all huddled in the middle of the room. My mom and sisters were trying to calm Luis down but were having no luck. Luis was frantically pushing and pulling us towards front door while uttering something about a man downstairs. In fact, when I yanked open the door that led into the kitchen, I think he thought I was the man, because it damn near gave him a heart attack.

Being the former ghetto dwellers that we were, as soon as we were able to decipher the words, "man downstairs," we got the hell out of that house pronto.

Our elderly neighbors, who spied us with distrust from the minute we moved in, were already sitting in front of their respective homes on brightly painted, highly glossed metal lawn chairs, and when they saw the five us come running out of the house, they scrambled for the safety of their homes leaving everything behind; in one case, a small yelping dog. I don't know who called the police but whoever it was, didn't call them to come help us, they called them to come get us.

Within minutes, a couple of Gary's finest came to a screeching halt right in-front of our house, followed by a second patrol car that did likewise in the alley directly behind our house.

The police officers approached us with caution and I believe the only reason why they felt safe enough to approach us at all was because they saw my mom and two sisters, otherwise I'm sure they would have immediately assumed that my brother and I were suspects and commanded us to get face down in the street.

I'll never forget that while we were trying to explain what was going on, the only thing they were interested in was how long we had been living in that house and how we came to be in that house in the first place. Keep in mind, back in 1974, West Glen Park was nearly all upper middle-class elderly white people, and we weren't any of those things.

Once the police determined who everybody was, they began to question my brother while they waited for more backup to arrive.

For nearly an hour, my brother Luis repeated his story as well as the description of the man he said was inside.

According to Luis, he was awakened by the noise of our neighbor cutting grass and while he laid in the dark, the light bulb directly above his head came on, and standing there, with his hand still on the string used to turn on and off the light was an old white man with white hair who looked to be anywhere from 85 and 95 years old.

After several more officers arrived, they walked around the house yanking on the basement windows and the back door, all of which were locked from the inside.

I didn't blame the cops for taking as much time as they did, after all, they were about to enter a house that they had never been in before, and search it, for what they believed was an intruder. I'm sure the only reason they didn't use a bull horn and order whoever was in the house to come out, was because the man my brother described was very old and they probably thought they were dealing with a case of dementia.

Finally, a plain clothed detective arrived, and he and two uniformed officers entered our house and searched it room by room. As they cleared each room on the main floor and then in the basement, a policeman would go to the window and give the cops outside the "thumbs up" to show that they were fine. They also posted a guard at the front and back doors to make sure that no one got passed them. In the end, they found nothing.

My father came home while all of this was going on and was naturally alarmed when he saw the police cars because he thought something bad had happened to one of us. But once he learned why the police were there, he didn't show any shock or concern. In fact, he didn't say much about it at all. Many years later I would learn why.

I don't know if my parents were ever billed for all of those cops coming to our house that morning, but they shouldn't have, because technically, we didn't call the police, someone else did.

For years the dreams persisted and Luis continued to see the old man but it always happened as he was coming out of a deep sleep so he came to believe that the man was the tail end of a dream.

For the next couple of years, a few weird things happened, but it wasn't until the summer of 1977 when something terrifying happened to me, that made me a true believer.

In 1977 I fell in love with a sexy hot babe from Merrillville High School who I met at the Y & W Drive-In on Broadway and things couldn't have been any better.

One night, I was in my basement bachelor pad, lying on my bed with my legs propped up against the wall, my head hanging off the edge of the bed and the telephone receiver pressed tightly against my ear so I wouldn't miss a word my gorgeous new girlfriend was saying.

The phone was mounted on the wall and had a real long cord that would get all tangled up so you'd have to let it dangle free to unravel itself. I hated those damn things but I was in love so nothing else mattered. But then something happened that did matter. With my head hanging off of the edge of the bed, I saw a small bench I had next to my desk move. It was a very slight move, but it moved.

The bench came with an electric organ my father bought for us from the old Sears on Broadway. It was light weight and cheaply constructed, basically four legs screwed into a half inch plywood board, with three inches of foam cushion for the seat, and covered with vinyl. Seeing it move didn't really scare me, because my three nephews were spending the night and they were always playing tricks on me.

I kept talking to my new love on the phone while I carefully and quietly slid off of the bed and positioned myself to pounce on my nephews. I jumped around the corner and screamed, "Got you!" But there was no one there to get. I remember my girlfriend saying, "You better believe you've got me," which made me chuckle and forget about everything else.

As I was explaining to her what was going on, I walked over to the door that separated my side of the basement from my brother's side, in order to lock the door from my side and put an end to my nephews' pranks. But the door was already locked from my side. I couldn't figure out what the heck was going on. I turned around to walk back to my bed and that's when I noticed that the bench which had been over to the left next to my desk was now directly in front of me, more importantly, directly between me and the staircase. Before my mind could fully accept what, I was looking at, the bench slowly slid about a foot towards me. Everything seemed to stop. Everything but the thumping of my heart which was now pounding so hard that I could literally hear it. My blood pressure rose so high that I thought my head was going to explode. My girlfriend kept saying something to me but to this day I have no idea what it was. And then the bench began trembling so violently that all four legs were off of the floor at the same time. And then the freaking thing levitated about four feet off of the floor, perfectly parallel to the ground, and just stayed there. Somewhere during all of this I went to my happy place. I have no idea how I got past the bench or how I made it up two flights of stairs, through the kitchen, through the dining room and into the living room, but I did.

My father was sitting on the floor watching TV. I have no idea what I said to him, but whatever it was, it was enough to make him run past me and down the stairs without asking any questions.

By the time I made it back downstairs my father was pounding the hell out of the bench with his fists. In the end, my father said that he saw nothing out of the ordinary. And added that the reason he was beating the crap out of the bench was to show me that it was just a stupid cheap bench.

It took a long time before I was able to sleep in my bachelor pad again, but being girl crazy and having your own private love pad is a strong detractor from the fears of the supernatural, so eventually life went back to normal and I never again experienced anything unusual.

Twenty years passed and one day I'm back in Gary with my wife and two children visiting the family and while sitting outside with my father he asked me if I remembered that night; as like if I could ever forget it. I thought he was going to make fun of me but what he said gave me the chills. He said that he wanted me to know, that when he walked into the basement that night in 1977, that the bench was pressed tightly against the ceiling. He told me that he had to literally pull the bench off of the ceiling and pound on it with his fist, just to get control of it. And that's when I walked into the room.

I asked my father why he hadn't told me this back then. His explanation was simple and honest. He told me that moving out of our old neighborhood, was a dream come true, and that he wasn't about to throw it all away over some playful ghosts who couldn't possibly hurt any of us. He was right, he was always right. If my father had told us what he actually saw back then, the entire family would have freaked out and moving was not an option.

In 2012 I researched the archives of the Gary Post, and found the old couple's obituaries along with the story of the old man's suicide. From the obituary it was easy to find their final resting place at the Oak Hill Cemetery only three blocks away from the house they called home for so many years.

It turned out that the couple had two sons, but unfortunately, they were both stillborn. The four of them are buried together.

Chapter Four

The Party Line

The Individual telling this story is Danny. Danny is a retired Army Officer who was born and raised in Gary and now lives in San Antonio, Texas.

The Party Line, which we learned about from the watching the television show *Happy Days*, was a telephone conference system accessible by dialing any same five numbers, from your home push button phone. The system was created so that first responders could talk to each other simultaneously during a natural disaster or other emergencies. In 1976 there was no such thing as conference calls, at least not for home use and we didn't have cell phones or Face Book, so the Party Line was a big freaking deal. The authorities had their uses for it and we had ours. And believe me, I spent many a happy hour on the Party Line, laughing and joking but mostly meeting girls.

A lot of real funny things happened on the Party Line, such as the time this hillbilly kid named Alvin got on and loudly demanded to know if there were any "jungle bunnies" on the phone. Alvin's hillbilly voice was unmistakable, especially in a place like Gary, Indiana. Nearly everyone on the phone that night save for the people from Merrillville and Hobart, knew immediately who he was and called him out by name.

"Thug," (not his real name but the only name we ever knew him by), shouted back, "White boy, I know who your dumb ass is, and I'm whooping your ass on Monday." Unbeknownst to any of us at the time, Alvin had dropped out of school. That and the fact that no one, not even Thug, was willing to wonder into Black Oak, ironically, Gary's only predominantly white neighborhood and where Alvin lived, gave Alvin all the bravado he needed to continue his taunts. So, for the next hour or so, Alvin annoyed everyone with racial slurs and stupid jokes. But, eventually someone at Alvin's house picked up a phone and screamed, "Boy get off of that damn phone!" That did the trick, he got off the phone and no one ever heard of him or saw him again.

The following Monday Alvin wasn't at school but that didn't stop the rumors from flying. One rumor claimed that Alvin got beat up at the bus stop and was taken to the hospital. Another rumor claimed that Alvin showed up at school with a bunch of inbred hillbillies and dared anyone to do anything. My favorite rumor was that Alvin drove up to the back of the school and when he saw Thug and some other black kids coming towards him, he pulled out a gun, put it to Thug's head, and made Thug beg for his life before climbing back into his car and speeding off.

Not everything that took place on the Party Line was silly kid stuff, often we'd engage in philosophical discussions regarding world events, advances in medicine, marriage and family, religion, sports and a bunch of other grown-up topics.

But more than anything else, the Party Line was where we went to "hook up," and I'm here to tell you, I hooked up a lot. I've always been partial to white girls, and the Party Line opened up a whole new world for me, more specifically, it gave me access to the elusive hamlet of Merrillville, Indiana and the Merrillville High School girls.

Nearly every adult living in Merrillville at that time where once Gary residences and without fail, every Merrillville kid I ever befriended, male or female was warned by their parents to stay out of Gary and never make friends with kids from Gary. Which was all the motivation they needed to do just the opposite. And the Party Line offered them a safe way to get their ghetto on.

Every night I was on the Party Line, but during the summer days I was at the West Glen Park Public Pool on 43rd Avenue across from the Oak Hill Cemetery.

I met my first real love Cindy at that pool and that's also where I learned that if you bent down and put your eyes parallel to the top of the towel drop off box in the boy's locker room, you could see directly into the girls' locker room.

My days were spent at the pool, my afternoons were spent learning about sex from Cindy who was two years older than me but my nights were spent on the Party Line.

There was a limit to the number of people who could be on the Party Line at the same time, so often, you'd have to dial in repeatedly until you were able to get on. But once you were on, it was a blast. A blast until your mom or dad picked up another phone at your house and embarrassed the crap out of you, by demanding to know, "Who the hell is on this phone?" And the kid whose house it was coming from would always hurry and hang up leaving their parents alone on the phone wondering who in the hell all of the people on the phone were.

Some parents knew about the Party Line and would listen in to make sure nothing bad was going on. Some parents were real cool and would politely announce, "OK, it's time to get off of the phone, I have to use it," allowing their kid, who naturally recognized their parent's voice, to save face and get off of the phone without any drama.

One time, this jock kid's life was ruined when his sister picked up the phone, addressed him by name, and politely said, "Mark, mom wants to know if you'll be off of the phone soon, because Dad needs you to run over to IGA and pick up some stool softener." Man did we howl! I laughed so hard I actually had an asthma attack. Luckily for the jock, it was summer and we were also transitioning from Bailey Jr. High to Lew Wallace High School, so when school resumed, he wasn't enrolled. According to rumor, after the phone incident, his family moved to Merrillville because the jock threatened to commit suicide if they didn't. I don't know how much of that is true, but he did graduate from Andrean Catholic High School on Broadway in Merrillville. Today he is a successful Pediatrician living in Indianapolis.

Each night I'd settle into my cozy bedroom for some late-night television watching, a couple of cold beers, a final "I love you" call from Cindy, and of course, the Party Line.

Around eleven o'clock one night, I got on the Party Line and was very disappointed to find only Thug and some woman on the phone. Thug was trying very hard to convince the woman that she should let him, "hit that," but she kept saying, "I got a man, he's just locked up right now."

After a few minutes I had heard all I could take from those two and was about to hang up, when I heard the distinct sound of someone else getting on the line. Thug didn't hesitate, in a flash he abandoned his carnal pursuit the woman he had been unsuccessfully courting and excitedly blurted out, "Who's that, who just got on the phone?" "What's up Girl?" Thug lived by the philosophy that if you throw enough crap at the wall, something will stick.

For about a minute, no one said a word. And then something said "hello," and every hair on my arms stood erect and I felt cold chills run down my back and my ears got really hot. I kid you not, it was the voice of a child, but not just any child, but a child out of a horror movie. And then the voice asked, "Who else is on the phone?" No one said a damn thing. After what seemed like an hour, I finally said, "I don't mean to be an asshole, but whoever you are, your voice is creeping me out." And I wasn't exaggerating. I actually jumped out of my bed and turned on the lights. Thug echoed my feelings and added, "Bitch you got me all scared and shit, why don't you get off the phone?" The woman Thug had been romancing didn't stick around to see how it turned out, her ghetto survival instincts were strong that night and she hung up without saying a word.

The person with the demonic kid's voice began to giggle hysterically which only scared us even more. Then the person apologized for having such a creepy voice and assured us that she was not a witch, not a demon, and not a child. She introduced herself as Teresa (not her real name), and explained that she had always had a little kid's voice. She said her parents thought her voice would change with age but it never happened.

According to Teresa, she was 29 years old, a lifelong resident of Gary and lived off of Ridge Road with her parents and a younger brother. She said she attended the small Glen Park School on 39th and Broadway and graduated from Lew Wallace High School. After a while her voice didn't scare us anymore and the three of us talked about a lot of things. Around one o'clock in the morning, Thug, wished us both a good night and hung up.

This might sound stupid, but what I remember most about that night, even after 40 years, was Thug's heartfelt goodnight to Teresa and I. I remember it as if it happened yesterday; Thug excused himself, and then said, "Yo man, I'm going to bed, have a real pleasant night, and Ma'am it was very nice meeting you and I'm sorry if I was disrespectful."

It's not unusual for a person to bid another person such a warm goodnight, but this was Thug saying this. Thug was about 19 years old; 6'ft 7inches tall, and easily weighed 270 pounds, all of which was muscle that he put on during long and numerous periods of incarceration. Aside from his impressive physical characteristics, he was mostly known for his propensity to commit criminal acts with or without violence. There was never a shooting that Thug was not the prime suspect in. To this day when I tell my friends and family this story, they have no problems believing that what I'm about to tell you actually happened, but they don't believe Thug ever said any of those things. For the record, he really did say those things.

Teresa was very nice and our conversation never drifted toward dating, or me "hitting that," not even about the two of us meeting. Besides, she knew that I wasn't even fifteen years old yet.

Around 3:00 AM, I bid her a friendly "good night" and got off of the phone. Around 3:15 AM, my phone rang. My mother knew that I was up all night playing around on the phone, so the phone ringing at that hour of the morning didn't alarm her, but I knew not to let it ring twice, so before the first ring stopped resonating, I jumped up and grabbed the receiver before it could ring again.

Much to my surprise, it was Teresa. She didn't apologize for calling my house at that hour, she just asked me if I wanted to meet her somewhere. "Hell, no I don't want to meet somewhere your scary ass bitch, how the hell did you get my number?" I didn't really say any of those things, but that's close to what I was thinking. What did say, was "Teresa, its going on four o'clock, how did you get my number?" She chuckled and said something like, "I have my ways," and then asked if I wanted to talk for a while. We talked for about an hour and then I bid her a good night again and promised to be on the Party Line later that night.

To teenage night owls, sunny mornings are a painful thing and that morning was no exception. I had only been asleep for two or three hours when the sound of my sister cutting the grass directly outside of my bedroom window woke me up.

The next thing I heard was my sister opening my bedroom door and whispering loudly, "There's a white lady on the front porch here to see you." Her voice contained the distinct sound of concern. She asked me if I knew who the lady was, and I said, "How the hell would I know, I haven't even seen who she is yet?" As I got dressed my sister cautioned me to be careful which freaked me out because she had never cautioned me to be careful about anything before.

Before stepping out onto the porch, I checked out the woman through the glass door. She was a woman alright, a white woman and from what I could see not bad looking either. She was wearing shinny purple skin tight disco pants, high heels and a white fluffy sleeved blouse. She looked harmless, but completely out of place for that early hour of the day. Her brownish blond hair which she would later describe as "mousy brown," was parted down the middle just past her shoulders and curled in the fashion of the day. She turned her head as I walked out to greet her, and that's when I got my first real good looked at Teresa. She wore blue eye shadow and long fake eye lashes. She looked like a cheap hooker, but a very attractive cheap hooker.

Teresa was very pale except for her face which was smeared with so much Cover Girl make-up that it made it several shades darker than the rest of her body. She stood up as she introduced herself which I found to be very classy. She wasn't a little kid at all, she was a full-grown woman, and as I may have mentioned before, a very attractive full-grown woman.

Teresa explained how she wasn't able to sleep so she found herself riding around and decided she'd stop by to meet me face to face. Even though I wanted to say something like, "If my mom wakes up and comes out here, she's going to be pissed," I acted like her being there was no big deal. I wanted so badly to know how she knew where I lived because I sure as hell didn't tell her, but more than that, I wanted her to leave before my dad got home from working the midnight shift. I played it cool, but I was stressed.

We made small talk and then she asked me if I'd like to go out sometime. She was going on 30 and I was going on 15. "Of course, I'd like to" I blurted out. After all, could you blame me? Think about it, I was a teenage boy just barely in high school, and she was a full grown very hot woman. I couldn't wait to tell my buddies about this.

As much as I liked where this was going, I had to get rid of her before my old man got home. Playing it as cool as I could, I told her that I needed to get some sleep because I had to help my brother with something later in the day. She was very sweet and apologized for waking me up so early and then leaned into me and gave me a light kiss on the lips.

I walked her to the street, excited to see what kind of car she was driving, after all, If I was going to date an older woman, I wanted her to drive nice car. But the only cars I saw were my neighbors' cars. Just as I was about to ask her where her car was, she reached over and grabbed the handlebars of a yellow ten-speed bike which was leaning against our wired fence, and without saying another word, she climbed aboard and peddled her sexy crazy ass down the street towards 45th Ave and she was gone.

After that morning, I didn't hear from Teresa again for almost an entire year so I just figured that she realized that I was way too young for her and moved on. I won't lie, I was disappointed, but I was also way too busy with my teenage life to dwell on it for very long, so I moved on.

And then, on another bright sunny summer morning I was awakened by my youngest sister Reagan, screaming "Wake up booty head, some girl is on the phone for you!" I should mention that by this time I had broken up with Cindy and was dating a girl named Kathy from Merrillville who I met on the Party Line.

I was insanely in love with Kathy; she was everything I ever dreamed of. She had her drivers' license, she lived alone with her mom who was never at home, she had big green eyes, and jet-black hair, she was gorgeous and if that wasn't enough, she had a great body too.

Anyway, I picked up the phone expecting it to be Kathy calling to remind me about our date later that night, but instead it was a strange and very sexy voice I had never heard before. The girl on the phone told me that we had never met but that she had seen me before and she thought I was foxy (the precursor to "fine as hell").

She described herself to me and I got excited. She asked me if I could meet her at the East Glen Park Little League Field which was about ten blocks away from my house. Having all the raging hormones of an all-American teenage boy, I never once stopped to ask her if we could meet at the West Glen Park Little League Field which was only four blocks from my house, and I also didn't stop to think once about Kathy.

Without hesitation, I quickly agreed to the meeting place and time and then called up my buddy Ricky and asked him to walk over there with me. I didn't really need any moral support, but I knew that girls always traveled in pairs and if things went the way I wished they'd go, I would need someone to keep the friend busy.

Ricky agreed and I hustled to get ready. As I was getting "dolled up," Kathy called and asked me what I was doing. I told her that I was getting ready to go with my dad over to Hammond to pick up something for his car and that I'd call her when I got back. Kathy sounded so sweet when she said, "I love you; I can't wait to see you." I told her that I loved her too and then finished getting ready from my blind date.

Ricky got to my house before I was ready and was equally excited over the strong possibility that the two of us might soon be getting "hooked up."

Glen Park was a nice place to live back then, so the thought of us running into any trouble was the furthest thing from either of our minds. But that's exactly what happen.

We approached the baseball field from the west so our view was of the back of the bleachers that faced east and towards the center of the baseball field itself. Although it was summer time, it was also a week day so there wasn't anyone at the field.

We didn't see the tanned colored station wagon parked on the opposite side of the field behind those bleachers facing west. In retrospect, I think I might have, but I must have figured it was the car the girl I was meeting was driving.

Ricky was the first to realize that we had walked into an ambush. It took a few seconds before my dumb ass realized it, but by then it was too late. I remember Ricky saying something like, "Ooooh shit," and I felt my blood ran cold and my stomach turn. How freaking stupid could I have been, I walked right into it. How did I not recognize that tanned station wagon? "You're busted you cheating bastard," a familiar voice shouted out. The tanned colored station wagon was Kathy's mother's station wagon, and sitting behind the wheel balling her eyes out was my girlfriend, Kathy. And standing outside of the car with her arms folded across her ample breast doing the name calling, was her best friend Kim.

Kim jumped back into the car and urged Kathy to start the car and drive away. But Kathy was crying so hard that she later told me that she didn't hear a word Kim was saying to her. I remember that morning as if it were yesterday, and one of the things I remember most, were the names that Kim was calling me, because I had never heard them before.

I was set up! I had been duped! Kim, who I would later cheat on Kathy with, let me have it the worse, "You douche, how could you?" I had never heard anyone called that before, and at the time, I didn't even know what a douche was. It was weird, she would insult me by asking herself questions like, "How did you ever get to be such a loser?" And then she'd answer her own question, "I'll tell you how, because he's vile," she said. "Vile," what the hell did that mean?"

As they were unleashing a barrage of foreign sounding insults on me, a voice inside of my head said, "Turn the tables on her." And that's exactly what I did too, I looked Kathy right in those big beautiful tear-filled eyes of hers and with the most accusatory and hurt tone I could muster, I stuttered, "I thought you, I thought you, loved me." I knew I was on the right path because they stopped cursing. Then I hit her with, "So this is how you express love in 'Merry Ville?" Without giving either of them a chance to respond, I said, "I started not to come here at all, and just let you sit and wait for me and never show up, but I wouldn't have missed seeing the look on your face for anything in the world." "You honestly thought I'd fail your stupid little test?" "I guess our kind needs to be tested." Then I hung my head low and walked off acting hurt. That was the one and only time in my life that I ever played the race card, but I had to, she had me by the short curlies.

Looking back, it's possible that I was the first person to ever play the race card. Either way, it worked beautifully. I shouted to Ricky, "Let's get the hell away from these two before they have us arrested for being "Spics" on a sunny day," and walked away fast.

Like I said, that shit worked beautifully, and before we had taken ten steps, Kathy and Kim were both begging, "Please don't," and "please come back." But now was no time to let the suckers off the hook, we had to play it all the way through. A true hustler never lets the "mark" know they've been hustled and if I was too eager to make up, they'd know I was conning them.

Since we were on foot and they had the car, we climbed onto the railroad tracks so they couldn't follow us, and made our way back across Broadway and into the west side. We didn't get off at my street because we knew they'd be parked outside of my house waiting on us. Instead we stayed on the tracks all the way to Grant Street and then strolled over to the Village for some Chuck Wheeler's Vienna Beef Red Hots. After all, we had to give them some time to think about what they had just done. While Ricky and I laid low, we thought hard about who could have set me up. What pissed me off more than anything was the fact that someone right at that moment was laughing their freaking heads off; but who?

Later that night I accepted a call from Kathy and she begged me to forgive her. She was really hot so I did and I also allowed her to come pick me up so we could keep our date at the Y & W Drive-In on Broadway as planned.

At the drive-in, she asked me to promise her that I really did believe it was her testing me. I could have ended it right there and then, but as I mentioned before, If I showed to much eagerness to put this behind me, she would have known that I was guilty of attempted cheating. So again, I turned it around and made her promise me, that she had not put one of her buddies up to test me. We promised each other and then we made up.

I survived the ambush, but I was still very angry and I began to suspect a lot of different people. It could have been any of my old girlfriends or any of her old boyfriends, or maybe it was one of her girlfriends who thought they were doing her a favor by splitting us up? Heck it might have even been Kathy's mom or her big sister who both hated me. For a very long time I couldn't stop racking my brain over who had set me up. But eventually I forgot about it and moved on.

Teresa came back into my life that fall. I don't know where she had been all of that time, but suddenly there she was, and she was not acting right.

It was a beautiful Midwestern day, the kind that you long for during the freezing wet winters and the scorching hot summers. I had already been cheating on Kathy with her buddy Kim for a couple of weeks before I finally broke it off with Kathy all together. I was such a jerk that the reason I gave Kathy for breaking up with her was that I simply couldn't get over the incident at the baseball field. Like I said, play it to the end. I wonder if she's going to read this?

It couldn't be helped; Kim was absolutely beautiful! She was five foot five inches tall, 115 pounds, blond hair, blue eyes, and the kind of body men have gone to war over. She was everything a man could ever dream of. And if that wasn't enough, she lived less than a block from my big brother Carlos' house in Merrillville.

By the way, if you're wondering if it ever occurred to me that it was Kim who set me up to get caught by Kathy at the Little League field, no, it never once crossed my mind. In fact, the first time I ever considered it was when I starting telling you this story. And that really blows too, because up until now, I was convinced that it was crazy ass Teresa who set me. I'll leave it up to you to decide who you think it was.

One Saturday morning, I woke up early, brushed my teeth, had some breakfast and walked to my brother's house in Merrillville. At my brother's house I visited with my sister-in-law and nephew until I knew it was safe to make my way over to Kim's house which was so close to my brother's back door, that I could literally see through the sliding glass door of her upstairs apartment. Ironically, Kathy use to live in that same apartment building before she and her mom moved to Crown Point.

Right about noon, Kim's mom took off with her boyfriend for the day and within minutes of them pulling out of the drive way, I was snuggled up with Kim in her bedroom. Unbeknownst to either of us, her father had made arraignments with her mother to pick Kim up and take her out for the day.

We were both passed out on her bed but luckily Kim had locked her bedroom door just in case her mom doubled back or her sister dropped by. I remember waking up to one of Kim's hands over my mouth while she used the other to point at her bedroom door. She whispered; "I think my mom came back." I quietly slipped off the side of her bed and rolled under it. Kim called out, "Who's out there?" And a man's voice replied, "It's a murderer."

She hung her head over the side of the bed and with eyes as big as saucers, said quietly, "It's my dad!" I was panic stricken, how in the hell was I going to get out of there? "Oh, if only it could have been a deranged killer," I thought to myself. There was no climbing out of her window without breaking some bones, and there was no back door because it was an apartment. The only way out of there was over the balcony or through the front door, and her father was directly in the path to both of those options.

Kim was scared but maintained an even strain. With me still under the bed, she put on some clothes, opened her bedroom and greeted her father with a big hug and a peck on the cheek. Kim obviously knew what to do to avoid suspicion, because when she opened her bedroom door, she opened it wide so her father could see the entire room.

Kim's father asked her if she had been sleeping to which Kim replied that she had dozed off while reading her book, which she actually had the sense of mind to place on her bed before she opened the door. Her dad walked over to the living room couch and told Kim that he was there to take her out to lunch and for her to go back to her book while he took a nap. Fast thinking as she was, she urged him to skip the nap and for him to freshen up while she changed clothes because she was really hungry and wanted to get back because her best friend Kathy would be coming over and they had plans to do something.

Kim shut her bedroom door and changed into some very tight Blue Jeans and a white flimsy "baby doll" blouse that was all the rage among the hippie types that year. I remember that Kim never wore a bra. I have no idea what that has to do with anything but it popped into my head so now you know.

As my mind went from, "How am I going to get out of here?" to "Wow, what a great body," we heard the water from hallway bathroom running. Her dad had taken her suggestion and decided to shave and brush his teeth so they could get going. Only problem was that he left the bathroom door wide open and I had to pass that bathroom door to get out.

Waiting until they left before I left was not an option because her father would set the alarm as he locked the door behind him.

Kim whispered to me, "I'll get him talking and you crawl past us." No sooner had I whispered back, "Are you freaking crazy?" Kim was standing at the bathroom door behind her father as he saved. Her father alternated between focusing on his shaving cream covered face and talking to Kim via the mirror, and when his attention was on his face, Kim would use her right hand to motion for me to 'come on," "stop," or "go back." And when he bent down to splash his face with cold water, Kim gave me a flurry of rapid "come on" hand movements, and as fast and as quietly as I could, I crawled past the open door, and made my way through the living room and down a very long flight of stairs to the front door and freedom.

Less than three minutes later, I was walking into my brother's front door where I was greeted by a very angry sister-in-law. Apparently, while I was reenacting a scene from *Escape from Stalag 17*, some "crazy bitch" named Teresa had been calling my brother's house looking for me. And when my sister-in-law refused to tell her where I was, she threatened to kick her ass.

What I was hearing freaked me out. That coupled with the fact that I had just escaped the clutches of a father who would have easily ripped my balls off and shoved them down my throat, pretty much had my head spinning. Although I assured my sister-in-law that I had no idea who Teresa was, I did know who she was.

Thankfully, Teresa never called back, but my sister-in-law stayed pissed off at me the entire day. I didn't want to walk back to Gary without seeing Kim again, so I did my best to calm her down. I played outside with my nephew all the while watching Kim's apartment for a sign of when I could go back over there but it never came.

After a couple of hours, I got bored and called my best friend Eddie who lived on the east side of Glen Park right behind Bailey Jr. High, to see what he was up to. Instead of hearing his customary warm greeting of "What's up fag?" I had my ass handed to me. The minute he heard my voice, he let loose with, "Hey asshole, what the hell's going on?" Apparently, some "crazy bitch" named Teresa had been calling his house all morning too, and when his mother told Teresa that she hadn't seen me in a couple of days, Teresa called her a lair and threatened her. Eddie was livid, he told me that I'd better get a hold of my bitches because they were out of control.

There was only one Teresa I knew, but for the life of me, I couldn't see Teresa doing anything like that, not to Eddie's mom or to my sister-in-law. It had to be an old girlfriend causing trouble. I tried hard to imagine the Teresa I knew, the older woman with the weird kid's voice from the Party Line who rode a boy's ten-speed bike doing something like that, but in the end I was convinced that it wasn't her, why would it be her, we never really got to know each other very well and it wasn't like we were dating.

After Eddie calmed down, he told me that this Teresa person started calling his house around eight o'clock that morning and at first, she was really polite to his mom who answered the phone each time she called. He told me that she even asked speak to him, so whoever this person was, knew his name. But after the fifth or sixth call, she became accusatory and started making comments like "So you're going to keep playing stupid?" In the end, she just came straight out threatened to come over to his house and show everyone what happens to people who "mess with her." I asked Eddie what she sounded like, and he screamed back, "Hell I don't know, like a bitch I guess, I never spoke to the hoe."

No sooner had Eddie and I hung up, that my brother Danny called to say that he was on his way over to pick me up and that I was in trouble. I hated not seeing Kim again, but I was more concerned about the trouble awaiting me at home; whatever it was.

When I got home, I was confronted with a very angry mother (my mother), and two equally angry older sisters. Everyone was pissed off over some woman named Teresa who kept calling the house making threats against them for allowing me to date a "whore." Before the day ended, even my oldest sister Marie who lived over on 42nd and Massachusetts was pissed at me for the same reason.

To keep from getting my ass kicked by my loved ones, I agreed that when Teresa called back, that I was to ask her to meet me at some secluded place where we could talk. And at this meeting, everyone was going to kick her ass. But it never came to that, because the calling stopped just as suddenly as it had started.

1978 started out horribly for me, Kim had left me for some college guy and her parents were OK with it because it got me out of her life. I was heartbroken beyond words, but what kept me going was my first real job at the KFC on Broadway next to the Glen Park School.

The first couple of months was rough on me because I had been very spoiled all of my life and I wasn't used to doing any real sort of work. But thankfully, unbeknownst to me, I had actually acquired a very good work ethic from my parents, and quickly made a reputation for myself as being a very hard worker. I was always at least 20 minutes early for work, I didn't horse around while on the clock, I never took anything that wasn't mine, I never once called in sick and I always stayed as long as they needed me to, which was all the time.

About two months into my job on a Friday night, myself, my supervisor, and one other co-worker were working the last shift, which meant we had to clean everything, balance out the cash register and then lock up the store. About an hour before we closed the phone rang and my supervisor answered it. She told me that I had a call but before she handed me the phone, she reminded me that employees were not allowed personal phone calls. I took the receiver expecting it to be my brother calling to see if I needed a ride home. But instead it was Teresa. She surprised the hell out of me and I wanted to know how she knew I worked there and why she was calling me. But my boss kept standing there with her arm extended waiting for me to hand her back the receiver so she could hang it up. All I was able to say was, "I can't talk now."

She said she understood and said, "You get off at 11, so meet me outside at the school playground when you get off." I wasn't that excited to hear from her, but I needed to get off of the phone so I said "OK."

The one thing you can count on when working the 3 to 11 shifts was never getting off at 11. We shut the doors at 10 PM but by the time we degreased and washed the floors and counters, filtered the hot grease to remove the "cracklings" we used to make the gravy, restocked everything, and balanced out the cash register, it was always after midnight, and this night was no exception.

When we finally did finish doing everything, we gathered in the lobby so we could set the alarm and all rush out together. But from the lobby's glass door we saw a commotion going on at the school across the alley which was less than 20 yards away. There were police cars everywhere and even a firetruck.

I kept looking over at the school for Teresa. I was concerned that something bad might have happened to her. A detective came over to us and asked if any of us had seen or heard anything suspicious going on at the school and after he was satisfied that none of us had, he told us that someone had shot at a homeless man. All I could think to myself was how lucky Teresa and I were that we weren't there when it happened. Teresa had obviously seen the commotion and was probably somewhere nearby waiting for me. I told my boss that I was going to hang out for a while but she would not hear of it, she told me that she was giving me a ride home and that was the end of it.

A couple of days later Teresa called me at home and she was furious. She said that she saw me walking down Broadway earlier that day and demanded to know why I didn't show up at the school the other night. But before I could begin to answer, she hung up on me. Her angry comments made no sense. It was as if seeing me suddenly reminded her that we never got a chance to meet at the playground that night and it pissed her off.

Several more months went by and I was hanging out at the pin ball place on 44th and Broadway. I loved that place. It was just one big room with a pool table in the middle and some pin ball machines, but it was the only thing like it in Gary as far as I knew. There was also a small "cloak room" in the back with a door that led to the alley where we would sit and smoke.

 One night, I was there playing pool when the owner called out my name and said, "You have a call." It scared me, because the only ones who knew I'd be there, were my family members, and if they were calling to find me, something really bad must have happened. Before the owner gave me the phone he said, "This is not a public phone, and next time you get a call I'm charging you a quarter." I apologized and asked him to please let me take the call because it had to be something serious. He reluctantly handed me the phone and to my relief and surprise, it was Teresa. She sounded agitated, and said, "You weren't at work, I called there and some witch told me you were off tonight; I'm going to get her." And then she said, "Come outside in ten minutes and I'll be there," and then she hung up. This is going to sound really stupid, but all I could think of at the time, was how cool I was going to look to all of the guys when they saw me with this older woman.

I went outside and smoked a cigarette while I waited for her. It was below freezing outside so before the ten minutes were up, I went back inside but stood by the window looking for her. Out of nowhere, the back door flew open and Thug and another guy we called Wetback, came flying in. They actually stumbled to the floor and were screaming "shut the door, shut the door." The owner went running back there to see what was going on, and Wetback said, "Someone is shooting at us." If you knew Wetback and Thug, it wasn't hard to imagine anyone shooting at them or them shooting at anyone. They said that they were standing outside smoking a "square," (a cigarette) more likely a joint, and they heard a bullet whiz over their heads. And before they could react, a second bullet whizzed past them. Believe me, those two knew exactly what bullets whizzing past sounded like. They said they had no idea where the shots came from and didn't stick around to find out. When the owner went to call the police, Thug and Wetback ran out the front door. Wetback was on house arrest and I think Thug was wanted at that time in connection to something; either way, neither of them wanted any part of talking to the police.

The police came out and asked everyone there a bunch of questions and looked around but after an hour or so, they left. The next afternoon, I stopped in there before going to work and I asked the owner's daughter if there was any news about the incident the night before. She was very excited and told me that the police were there first thing that morning and found two bullet holes. She showed me one bullet hole about five feet above the back door and a second one that hit the wall about a foot off of the ground just left of the door. If someone was trying to kill either of those guys, they sucked, because neither of those shots came close to hitting them.

The owner's daughter surprised the hell out of me when she told me that the police wanted to ask me some questions. I told her that was there at the time, but that I only knew as much as anyone else. She apologized and then said, "You look just like the Puerto Rican guy they call Wetback." I hadn't thought about it before, but Wetback and I did look a lot alike. We were both Hispanic, both dark skinned, we had the same build, we were the same height, we both had long black hair, and we both wore the same identical maroon colored winter jacket with imitation lamb fur around the collar. I remember saying to the girl, "You just scared the shit out of me, I sure as hell hope that whoever is trying to shoot Wetback doesn't mistake me for him and shoot me instead."

A couple of weeks after the pin ball place incident, I was telling a group of guys about that night and my buddy Ricky asked, "Are you sure someone didn't mistake Wetback for you?" We all laughed, but Ricky wasn't laughing, and he wouldn't let up, he asked me if it had ever occurred to me that this Teresa person may be trying to kill me. I told him that he was full of crap and I went off to work. But later that night when I was walking home from work, I started thinking about it, and I got scared.

Teresa did ask me to meet her in the school yard the night someone shot at the homeless man. In fact, he was probably sitting where I would have been waiting for her. Was that why she was so pissed off when she saw me walking down Broadway a couple of days later? And at the pin ball place, when she didn't see me standing in front of the building, did she circled around and when she saw Wetback standing behind the building assume it was me and opened fire? I was naïve, young and horny, so it took me a while to catch on to things, especially when it came to girls, but suddenly it was obvious to me, Teresa wanted to kill me and I had no idea why.

As much as I wanted to run to my parents or to the police, I was a man, and telling on a woman because she scared me, would have ruined me for life. Instead, I did what any real macho man would do; I worried all of the time, I watched my every step, and jumped whenever the phone rang or whenever anyone knocked on our door.

I never heard a word from Teresa again, but a couple years later, I was walking between classes at Lew Wallace High School, when a guy I had known since we were in grade school together, cornered me in the staircase and asked me why I was saying stupid things about his sister trying to kill me. He reminded me that we were friends, but made it very clear that if I didn't stop talking bad of his sister, that he was going to beat my ass. I had no idea what he was talking about, and then it hit me, his last name and Teresa's last name were the same. I was absolutely speechless. It took a few minutes, but after a while I was able to stutter, "Teresa is your sister?" He pushed me hard against the wall and through clinched teeth said, "You know damn well she's my sister."

He could have easily wiped the floor with me, but instead, he was the one in distress. I should have been the one in fear for my life, but he was the one that looked like he was about to fall apart. The whole incident was surreal. To the other kids who walked past us, we must have looked like two gay lovers breaking up, because at one point, when I attempted to ask him about Teresa, he very gently but very firmly clasped my face between his hands and pressed his forehead against mine. He didn't say anything for a good two minutes which made things look even worse. And then he said, "Asshole, my sister died in 1974."

He told me that his sister had suffered from some sort of mental illness for many years before she died. And then explained how not long before she died, she had seen our sixth-grade class picture, and even though I was around twelve years old at the time, and she had already graduated from high school, she became obsessed with me. He said that their parents forbade her from making any attempts to meet me because I was way too young. He didn't tell me how she died, only that she died early in 1974 in her upstairs bedroom. If this was true, she died more than a year before I met her.

I don't know if my friend was just trying to protect his sister and Teresa was still alive or if this whole thing was just one big joke from the very beginning. But I'll be honest with you, even to this day, sometimes when I hear my wife answer the phone, I listen nervously until I know who she's talking to.

Chapter Five

A phantom train?

The person telling this story is Fidel, a former resident of Gary who retired from the U.S Navy and works as a VA nurse in Maryland.

I loved a lot of things about growing up in Northwest Indiana, among them, was being able to go just about anywhere at any time and have fun even if you were under 21. It's been more than 40 years ago, but I'll never forget one Friday night when three of my buddies and I were headed to the South Side of Chicago for a night of drinking and dancing but almost ended up in the Twilight Zone.

Like I said, it's been more than 40 years since this happened so I might not remember every detail, but to the best of my knowledge, here is what happened.

It was right about ten o'clock at night when we started out for our favorite club on the South Side of Chicago. We knew all of the back roads, so it typically took us no more than 45 minutes to get there.

We left my buddy Alfredo's house on 50th and Washington in Gary's Glen Park neighborhood, traveled up Broadway, then west on Ridge Road, and then we turned north on either Clark Road or Burr Street. I'm not clear on which street it was, not because it happened so long, but rather because I had already been drinking for hours before the incident happened.

I do remember that we were driving through Brunswick when we came up on some cars stopped at a railroad crossing at I believe 9th Avenue. I also remember the crossing guards were already down but the caution lights were not blinking on and off and the caution bells weren't ringing.

We were probably the ninth or tenth car in line and from the rear left passenger's seat I could clearly see the line of cars on the opposite side of the tracks that were also stopped and waiting for the train to pass.

We sat in our car planning the night ahead and after a minute or two, the red caution lights began to blink on and off and the caution bells began to clang and then we saw the light from the locomotive approaching from the right. The ground began to vibrate from the weight of the train as it approached the crossing directly in front of us. However, in spite of the incredible noise the train was making, it became obvious to everyone that there wasn't a train anywhere in sight. We could hear the train and we could even feel the train, but there wasn't a train anywhere.

People on both sides of the tracks began to pour out of their cars and make their way towards the railroad tracks. There had to be at least 20 or 30 people staring directly at one another from opposite sides of the tracks with absolutely no earthly idea of what the hell was going on.

As something past directly in front of and in between the large crowd of people who had gathered, it stirred up enough wind so that those of us closest to the tracks had to shield our faces. We never heard the train's horn, but one could clearly hear that metallic clicking sound that only a moving train makes as it rocks back and forth. But again, there was no train.

The experience was surreal and it went on for at least two minutes. And then, it just stopped. It didn't fade away slowly, it just stopped. The crossing arms went up, the lights stopped flashing, the bells stopped clanging, and all that was left were a bunch of scared people standing on a dark street staring directly at one another from opposite sides of those railroad tracks.

People at the very back of the line in both directions who had not experienced the phantom train began to honk their horns until finally everyone got back into their respective cars and began to drive. Some people continued to wherever it was they were going before it happened, but others, either too shook up to go on, or maybe they just wanted to talk with others about what they had experienced pulled their cars over to the side of the road and began to gather.

As creepy as the incident itself was, what scared me the most was having to cross over the tracks. To me it felt as if we were crossing over into a place where dead things were.

The whole thing unnerved us so much that we only made it as far as Main Street in East Chicago Harbor where we decided that maybe we'd better call it a night; even though it wasn't even 10:30 yet.

We walked into a Mexican restaurant that was already closed but still had some customers sitting at tables. We ignored the waitress when she told us that they were closed and sat down. Right behind us entered an older couple and the woman was freaking out over the same incident we had just experienced.

Restaurant staff hurried over to them to see what was wrong with the woman, so we walked over to them as well and explained that we had just come from the same place and had experienced the phantom train ourselves. The woman jumped out of her seat and grabbed me by my shirt, practically ripping it off of me. She demanded that I tell her that it was all part of a joke. Her husband pulled her off of me and apologized. I told him that I was sorry for upsetting his wife but assured them both that if it were a joke that we had nothing to do with it.

Before long, nearly everyone who worked in the restaurant and the Mexican market that was attached to it, gathered around our table just to hear the story. People were literally sitting on the floor crossed legged hanging on every word we said. It created such a commotion that people began coming over from the dance hall across the street.

Before long two East Chicago police officers showed up because someone had reported a disturbance. Once the police were satisfied that there was no disturbance, they listened to us repeat what we had experienced and then left. But when their shift ended, they both came back and we all ended up drinking with them and the restaurant staff for hours.

As scared as we already were, after the police officers shared with us some of the scary things that they had experiences over the years, everyone was too scared to leave and go home. And when we did leave, we took the most indirect route home, just to avoid the area.

That was a long time ago and to this date, no one has yet been able to explain to me what we experienced that night.

Author's comment: While researching Fidel's claims, I found a story about a troop train that collided with a circus train on a set of tracks that went right through Brunswick pretty much parallel to 9th Avenue.

Although the accident is best known as the Hammond Circus Train Wreck, the accident actually occurred at a point officially known as Ivanhoe Interlocking, in Gary, about five and half miles east of Hammond. And the tracks on which the accident occurred, cross over both Burr Street and Clark Road in Gary's Brunswick neighborhood.

The train wreck occurred in June of 1918 and over eighty people were killed, many of them were burned beyond recognition.

Is it possible that the thing Fidel and his friends experienced that summer night in 1978 was the that troop train in route to a collision that occurred 60 years earlier?

Chapter Six

The dead lady outside of Lew Wallace High School

The person telling this story is Richard. Richard was born in East Chicago and raised in Gary. He is a professor of Criminology and currently lives in Florida.

It was about ten in the morning when I set out for school, I don't remember why I was late for school that morning, I only remember that I was. It had snowed throughout the night so when I walked out of my front door and onto our front porch the snow was as high as the third step. I remember that the sky was a very dull cobalt blue and if it wasn't for being the dead of winter, I would have bet money that a severe thunderstorm or maybe even a tornado was on its way. I always thought that those Indiana winter mornings were beautiful and I guess I still do. Except for the one I'm about to tell you about.

My routine was always the same, I'd walk out of my front door, hit the sidewalk and take a left. No more than the length of a football field from my house was 45th Avenue, and immediately on the other side of 45th Avenue was my Alma Matta, Lew Wallace High School.

On this particular morning, for reasons I cannot remember, instead of keeping to my routine, I hit the sidewalk, and turned right, and at the corner, I turned left and at the next corner which was Monroe Street I turned left again, which led me directly towards the school's brown gymnasium doors.

The snow was deep and my platform shoes offered no protection from the wet snow nor did my bell-bottom pants which were fanned out and literally froze that way.

From a distance, I saw a wall of snow created by a snow plowing truck that had earlier cleared 45th Ave. Stopped directly in front of the snow wall, at the intersection of Monroe and 45th Ave was a dark colored 1960s model idling car. The white smoke from the exhaust combined with the blinding white snow made it nearly impossible to see much of the car, let alone anyone inside of the car.

The snow plows that cleared 45th Ave had also cleared the side streets too, and whenever they did that, the snow would pile five feet high on either side of the one-way streets and would often completely bury any cars that were left parked there the night before.

I didn't feel safe squeezing past an idling car especially since I didn't know who was in it, but I had no choice. I approached the car cautiously, while also trying very hard to be as noisy as I could so I wouldn't spook whoever was in the car and get shot.

As I made my way through the cloud of smoke exhaust that surrounded the car, I noticed that the driver was a white woman with long brown hair. In 1976, Caucasians in Gary's Glen Park neighborhood wasn't a rare thing to see, so I had no reason to think anything about it.

However, the car wasn't stuck in the snow and it wasn't broken down, so why she was just sitting in it made no sense. I'm not sure if this is important or not, but Monroe Street is a one-way street and the car was facing the wrong way.

I don't remember if the idea of offering to help the woman ever entered my mind, but when I looked into the car, it was obvious to me, that the woman in the car was dead. Not at all an unusual sight in Gary, but in Glen Park back in 1976, it was.

It wasn't as if I'd seen a lot of dead people before, but this was unmistakable, this poor lady was dead. Her body was behind the steering wheel and her head had fallen forward so that her chin was resting on the steering wheel and her eyes were wide open. Her mouth was slightly open and there was bloody saliva hanging frozen from her bottom lip. I was scared, but I was fixated on her face. More than anything else, I remember her face.

Even though I was less than 30 feet away from the school, I might as well have been alone on the moon, because there was nobody anywhere around. There were no sounds, there were no signs of life anywhere, there was nothing. There were houses everywhere, but they were all locked up with their drapes drawn tight. I tried to run from the car and make it across 45th Ave but that was impossible because of that damn wall of snow in front of me. I fell flat on my face twice but finally managed to crawl up to the top of the hill. As I was laying there completely out of breath, I could see kids moving around inside of the gymnasium directly in front of me but no one inside of the school was paying attention to anything going on outside. I looked back at the car which was no more than 10 feet behind me and about four feet below me, and that's when I got the shock of my life. The dead woman wasn't in the car anymore, she was now standing outside of her car. Her face had no color save for the frozen blood on her face, and she just stood there staring at me. It was surreal and I was scared shitless.

I let myself roll down the opposite side of the snow hill and directly onto 45th Ave. From my new position, the car was no longer visible nor was the woman. I crawled, ran, and dragged myself across 45th Ave to the gymnasium doors and banged on them for dear life. The coach opened the door and screamed at me to use the side entrance but I pushed passed him and collapsed onto the wood floor. He thought I was suffering from over exposure and screamed for someone to go get the nurse. I was freaking out. It took a long time before I was finally able to mumble, "There's a dead lady in a car over there." Everyone in the gym began to freak out.

The resource officer showed up and immediately called for back-up but in the meantime, he braved the weather alone and made his way across the street to see for himself. He found nothing. No woman, no car, no sign of there ever being a car there; nothing. He cancelled the back up and escorted me to the principal's office. They read me the riot act and insisted that I tell them who put me up to making up the story. In the end, they were convinced that it was all some freshman hazing prank and that I was too afraid to tell them who made me make up the story.

The only other possible answer was that the poor woman had driven directly into the snow wall, knocked herself unconscientious, and before the resource officer made it to the scene, the woman came to and simply backed her car down Monroe Street and left.

Maybe that was exactly what had happened, the woman had driven directly into the snow wall and hit her head on the steering wheel and knocked herself out. Maybe, when I saw her standing next to her car, she had simply woken up and climbed out of her car looking for help. The only problem with that story is that I knew that she had not collided with the snow wall, there were at least ten feet between the front of the lady's car and the snow wall.

Looking back to that winter, none of us knew that we were living through the blizzard of 1976 and I also didn't know that that incident was just the beginning of a lot of dead people suddenly appearing and disappearing in that neighborhood.

Chapter Seven

Next time call a freaking tow truck!

The person telling this story is Jay. Jay grew up in Gary and is now a U.S. Government Procurement Officer living in Kentucky.

It was the Blizzard of 76 and I was working at a snack bar at the South Lake Mall in Merrillville just south of Gary. What started out as a simple act of helping a friend with car trouble turned out to be something right out of *The Night Gallery*.

Gordon and I were literally in the hallway behind the store locking up for the night when the phone rang. I went back inside and answered it and to my surprise, it was one Al, one of our high school buddies asking for help. The connection was really bad but I was able to make out that he was broken down off of Burr Street, near the store "This Is It."

Al was known to go the extra mile to "hook up," but the neighborhood of Black Oak was way off the grid, even for him. Not to mention, we were in blizzard conditions.

I knew where Burr Street was and I knew where "This Is It" was, but that was all I knew about that neighborhood.

By the time we left the mall it was pushing midnight and it had to be twenty degrees outside, which gave us even more incentive to find Al as soon as we could. As urgent as the situation was, we could only move at a snail's pace because the road conditions and visibility were really bad.

Gary isn't like other cities, there are no 7 Elevens, diners or convenience stores anywhere. At best, there might be a gas station open, but not the kind you can walk into for shelter.

It's been a real long time so I don't remember the names of streets but I do remember that we ended up somewhere west of Burr Street on a road that ran parallel to the expressway. What I'm about to tell you next should be the climax of the story but it's only the beginning.

About half a mile from where we turned off of Burr Street, we drove up on the body of a naked man lying stiff on the road. We didn't get out of the car to check on his condition, but we were certain that he was dead. We turned off our radio to better concentrate on what we were looking at, and we turned on our high beams, but that was the extent of what we were willing to do. We were not about to get out of the freaking car.

If that had happened today, we would have immediately used our cell phones to call the police, but they didn't exist back then, so all we could do was keep driving and try and find a pay phone and call for help. We kept reassuring each other that wherever the pay phone was, is also where we would find Al.

I carefully drove my small blue Pinto station wagon past the body careful not to run over the corpse's extended arm. Believe me, we weren't insensitive to the poor dead guy, but there was nothing we could do. And besides, it was below freezing, it was too dark to see anything, and we were scared shitless. No matter how you looked at it, there was nothing we could do to help this guy, so we drove off to find help.

We drove up and down a couple of streets and got lost. We tried to make it back to Burr Street or to find Colfax

Street, but we kept running into dead ends or impassable snow-covered streets.

Black Oak, at least back then, was sparsely populated, and any hope it ever had of being developed beyond what it already was ended when they put Interstate 80 and 90 through it, literally separating it from Glen Park, which back then was the nicest part of Gary.

Driving through Black Oak back then was like driving through rural areas of West Virginia; they had a slaughter house, a rodeo, a mud track for dirt bike racing and lots of open fields for hunting rabbits and the best fishing holes anywhere. And there were farm animals everywhere too. All of that was kind of strange considering that we were no more than 30 miles from Chicago's city limits.

Black Oak also had a lot of isolated roads where unwanted appliances, furniture and stolen cars often ended up not to mention the occasional homicide victim.

If I remember correctly, there was a small baseball field between where we were and the highway. And that's where our car got stuck on the snow. Not in the snow, but on the snow. No matter how much we tried, we couldn't free the car because I had driven up onto a snow pile and we weren't going anywhere.

Imagine the scenario, two guys in a blue Pinto station wagon, in below freezing temperature, with snow falling so heavy that the roads are literally disappearing right before our eyes, and not a living creature in sight. Oh, and we had just found a naked dead guy in the street.

We sat in the car until the cold became too much for us to handle. We were within rock throwing distance from the highway, but not even the salt trucks were willing to chance the road that night.

At about 2 am, out of desperation and a real fear of freezing to death, we decided to start walking back towards Burr Street and hopefully find help. I wasn't familiar with the area, but I knew that as long as I kept the highway to my right, Burr Street was directly in front of us.

Almost immediately we realized that this may have been a fatal decision. The wind began to blow from every direction so hard that we couldn't even see the car we had just walked away from. After what seemed like an hour of walking, we
spotted lights in the distance and we made our way towards it with every ouch of strength we had left. The lights were coming from a house with a covered front porch. We knew that this was our one and only chance for survival. Even if we had to break into the house and get arrested, we had to get into that porch.

As we got closer to the house, we realized that it was the same street where we had found the naked dead guy. "Great" I thought to myself, in spite of all of our efforts to distance ourselves from the dead guy we ended up right back where he was.

If there was ever any doubt before that the guy was dead, there wasn't anymore because he was still laying in the street only now, he was partially covered with snow. But at that moment, our focus wasn't on the dead guy, it was on saving our lives, so with our heads down, we rushed up the steps of the house and began to pound on the door. Immediately the porch light went out.

We banged and begged and screamed for someone to please let us in or at least call the police, and then finally, a very large and angry Hispanic man holding a shot- gun opened the door to the house and stepped into the porch. The man, who we'll call Richard, asked through the locked porch door, "What the hell do you want?" We stood there shivering so hard that I thought my teeth were going crack. The snot from my nose had literally frozen across my lips, making it nearly impossible for me to open my mouth. Finally, he unlocked his porch door took a few steps backwards and yelled for us to come into the porch.

He kept his distance from us and he never lowered the shotgun. After a few minutes, I was finally able to explain to him how we got stuck in the snow while looking for a buddy who was broken down somewhere nearby and that while looking for him, we found a dead man, who by the way, was lying in the street right out there in front of his house.

This is going to sound stupid, but as I was waiting for him to either shoot us or tell us to get the hell out of his house, I remember thinking to myself, "I didn't know there were Mexicans living in Black Oak, I thought it was all Hillbillies."

And then Richard's eyes bugged out and he screamed, "What in the hell!" I immediately thought to myself, "Oh great, he just noticed the dead guy in the street out in front of his house and he thinks we killed him." When I turned to point towards the dead guy and offer something in the way of "Sir, that's how we found him," I saw that the naked dead guy wasn't there anymore.

Gordon said something like "au hell naw!" and in a flash, Richard grabbed me by the collar of my jacket and yanked me into the house all the while shouting, "Get in the damn house, get in the damn house!" I literally fell into Richard's house with Gordon landing on top of me.

I was in the middle of begging him to believe that we didn't do anything to that man, but before I could finish, we saw the dead man's face pressed tightly against the small triangular window in the center of Richard's front door. The same door we had just entered through.

The dead man's eyes were wide open and frantically moving from left to right as if scoping the room for a way to get in. And then it started pounding on the door and jiggling the door knob.

Gordon was freaking out! Richard was screaming for us to "shut the f--- up!" I crawled out of the way and joined Gordon who had crawled into the living room and was huddled up next to the couch.

Richard kept the shotgun pointed at the door until the pounding stopped. As we sat there staring at Richard who was positioned to shoot whatever came through the door, our concentration was broken when we all saw the dead guy walk slowly past Richard's living room window. He didn't look into the house, he just looked straight ahead as he walked past. We kept asking Richard, "What the hell is going on?" But all Richard said was "Shut up," then ran to the door at the far-right side of his living room. And just as he reached that door, the man began to pound on it.

After a few seconds the pounding on that door stopped and Richard ran past us again but this time he ran into his kitchen where his back door was. No sooner had he reached that door that man or thing, began to pound on it. I remember that during the entire ordeal, a dog that I hadn't noticed before, was running with Richard from room to room. It's not an important detail, but it was so strange how the dog never once barked or paid any attention to Gordon or to me.

As Richard guarded the back door, Gordon and I bravely inched our way towards the living room window hoping to see any form of help, and that's when we realized something that nearly stopped our hearts.

The bottom of Richard's living room window was at least five feet off of the ground outside. So, if anyone were outside trying to look in, all you'd see of them would probably be their heads or maybe their heads and shoulders. In other words, there was no way that we could have seen the entire figure of the dead guy pass the window, but that is exactly what we all saw.

When the pounding on the back door stopped, Gordon and I clearly saw the entire form of a man standing outside of the living room window. But it wasn't the naked dead guy, it was another man, and he wasn't naked, he was fully dressed in a suit, like a mortician would wear.

I don't remember much after that except for Richard physically restraining Gordon from trying to run out of the front door and Gordon completely losing it.

Somewhere during the hysteria someone or something outside screamed real load. It wasn't a blood curdling scream it was the sound of man hollering "Hey!" That's when we finally saw exterior lights from some of other houses come on and the muffled sounds of dogs barking.

Apparently, whatever it was had gone and Richard knew it, because he stopped running from door to door and pretty much collapsed on the floor next to us.

I'm not joking, Gordon and I were in shock; we didn't know what to do or what to say because we were that scared. Richard sat on the floor with his face in his hands and without ever looking up, calmly told us to help ourselves to whatever he had in the refrigerator. After a few minutes, he lifted his head and pointed outside and said "It stopped snowing, give me a few minutes and I'll walk back with you to your car and help get you unstuck."

But Gordon and I couldn't calm down, not even after Richard assured us that everything was alright. For a long time, the three of us and the dog just sat on his living room floor. After a couple of shots, a joint and a few beers, we finally calmed down and began to laugh and even cry a little.

We were very grateful to Richard for saving our lives, but we demanded to know what the hell had just happened. All Richard would say is that he grew up in that house, and that the man we saw lying in the street had appeared several times since he lived there. He said that although it was certainly terrifying, as far as he knew, no one had ever been harmed by it. And then he added, "But then again, it's never gotten inside anyone's house." No matter how much we begged him to tell us what it was, he insisted that he knew nothing more about it. And what about the second man we saw? Richard had no idea what we were talking about, or at least he said he didn't. In the end, Richard was the guy holding the shotgun so we decided to let it go.

Before long, the sounds of salt trucks could be heard making their way up and down the highway. Even though it was still pitch-black outside, we walked down to our car with some shovels and got it unstuck.

Because the street had nearly a foot of snow covering it, Richard and Gordon followed me on foot as I drove the car to Burr Street, several times pushing it when the tires wouldn't make traction. Before long we had made it across the overpass and back to the safety of Glen Park.

It was about 6 AM, when we finally made it to my house and the first thing, we did was call Al to see if he was OK. I can't tell you how relieved we were when he answered the phone. As I was trying to explain to him what we had gone through while looking for him, he interrupted me with, "Man calm down, first of all, I never called you last night, and second, I haven't left my house in two days."

Over the past 37 years I've driven people to where it all happened now and again, but I've never knocked on Richard's door or attempted to have him validate my story. I don't know why, but I don't think he would.

Chapter Eight

Ray's big spooky house

The person telling this story is Eric. Eric retired from the Gary School System after 30 years and currently lives in the Dayton, Ohio.

I was staying at my friend Ray's house one school night because we had procrastinated so long on a science project that we were forced to stay up all night and complete the project before class the next morning.

At approximately 10:30 PM, Ray and I were sitting in his third-floor bedroom, gluing pictures we had cut out of magazines onto a poster board. We were concentrating on putting the finishing touches on our project, when something or someone started pounding on the floor just a few feet from where we were sitting. At first, we weren't sure what we heard, because we had the radio playing pretty loud and we were also singing along to Ray, Goodman and Brown's latest hit "Special Lady." But the knocking grew so loud that it became difficult for us to concentrate on the music and we could even feel the vibration with each loud thump.

Ray turned down the radio, then walked over to his bedroom door and yelled down, "Sorry Ma," thinking that his mother was banging on the ceiling for us to turn down the music. When she didn't answer, I looked over at Ray and asked, "What is she using to reach the ceiling?" Ray looked at me and asked, "What the hell are you talking about?" I reminded him that the ceilings in his house were at least 15 feet high. Ray stared at me for a few seconds then bolted down the stairs to see what was going on. I ran over to the top of staircase and stared down at Ray as he slowly opened the door to his parents' bedroom which was on the second floor. He stuck his head in and whispered, "Is everything alright?" When neither or his parents respond he looked up to me and shrugged his shoulders.

Ray was making his way back up the stairs when the knocking started again. It wasn't anywhere near as loud as it was before, but it was definitely coming from his room. Suddenly Ray's parents walked out of their bedroom and scared the crap out of us. They weren't very happy and demanded that we'd stop doing whatever it was we were doing. We assured them that we weren't doing anything and asked them if they had been knocking on the ceiling. Too tired to even entertain our question, they shouted, "Go to bed!" and then turned and went back into their bedroom.

I waited for Ray to get back up the stairs and then we cautiously creeped into his bedroom to look for source of the knocking. The entire time we were searching his room, the knocking persisted. It wasn't as loud as before and it didn't appear to be coming from the floor anymore either. We stood in the middle of the room and moved our heads from side to side scanning the room for the source of the knocking and that's when we zeroed in on it. It was coming from the window. We looked at each other and then very carefully moved towards the window. We were cautiously creeping towards the noise when Ray grabbed my arm and mumble, "There is nothing outside of that window." From the corner of my mouth, much like a ventriloquist might do, I asked, "How do you know that?" Ray, did his own very poor impression of a ventriloquist and mumbled back, "We're on the third floor." Damn, he was right! There was no way anyone could be knocking on that window unless they were standing at the top rung of an extremely high ladder. It's important for me to point out, that the knocking wasn't on the glass, but rather on the wood frame, or the exterior wall around the window.

We inched our way towards the window and then strained our necks to see beyond the windowsill and then the knocking stopped. We pressed our foreheads against the window pane and looked straight down, the way you do when looking out of an airplane window to see the ground below you. There was nothing outside of or below that window. Being on the third floor, we had an unobstructed view for blocks, but all we saw was sky, roof tops, and the street below. We looked up then down and left and then right and we saw nothing. But before either of us could say anything, whatever was responsible for the knocking, slammed an unseen open palm on the glass window pane and we screamed bloody murder. It sounded just as if someone had bounced a big beach ball as hard as they could against the window without breaking the glass. I am not exaggerating when I say that we lost our composer. We jumped so high that I'm surprised we didn't break an ankle when we landed. Ray's screams rivaled anything ever performed by the late great Jackie Wilson.

After regaining ourselves, we convinced each other that a bird must have lost its way in the dark and slammed into the window. We laughed and then went downstairs to assure Ray's parents that there was nothing wrong but again, they were fast asleep.

Everything quieted down and we finished our project and dozed off, me on a chair and Ray on the floor. But around 4:30 AM, we were awakened by the sound of Ray's mother calling out "who's there, what do you want?" and Ray's dog, who was going absolutely nuts.

We ran down two flights of stairs and found Ray's mother standing at the entrance of their kitchen staring directly at their back door which led out onto a covered porch. We heard the porch door slam shut as if someone had opened it and then allowed it slam shut. Ray ran past his mother and turned on the porch light. From where we were standing, we could look through the kitchen window and directly into the porch, and saw nothing and no one.

Ray's father was in the adjacent room staring out of the window and from there, he could see the porch door from the outside. Seconds after we heard the porch door slam shut, he literally walked into the kitchen where we were and without ever looking at us, mumbled, "There was no one there." And then calmly said, "Call the police," and sat down at the kitchen table.

The police got there fast and did a real good search of the outside of the house. When they were done, they walked over to Ray's parents and reported that they couldn't find anything out of the ordinary.

By the time the police left, it was too late for any of us to go back to sleep so Ray's mom made us breakfast while Ray's dad conducted another search of the house.

After breakfast Ray's father drove us to school and to no one's surprised, Ray's mother came along for the ride. Ray later told me that his dad stayed home from work that day because his mom refused to stay there alone.

Chapter Nine

My murdered girlfriend

The person telling this story is Dennis. Dennis grew up in Gary, and today is a professor or Health Care Administration and lives in a very exclusive community outside of San Antonio, Texas.

In the first half of the 1980s my ex-girlfriend and her best friend were raped, mutilated and murdered.

It's been over 30 years, but there's times when I wake up in the middle of the night or even to a bright sunny day and I have to remind myself that it wasn't just a bad dream, it really did happen; but it happened a real long time ago.

To Gary natives, violence, even murders are more common than fatal car accidents. But murder typically came from of a gunshot; never from being tortured and mutilated.

But in 1985 all of that changed when my neighbor Ruth Pelke was stabbed 33 times by some girls from Lew Wallace High School. As horrific and ghastly as that was, it wasn't as sadistic and prolonged as the murder of my ex-girlfriend and her best friend. I'm not trying to down play what happened to Mrs. Pelke I'm just saying that thankfully she wasn't forced to watch her friend get dissected, knowing that she was next.

The details of my ex-girlfriend's murder are disgusting and unimaginable and each time I think I can talk about them I get very sick to my stomach. It's the same sick helpless feeling that I felt in Iraq when the sand storms came in and the mortars started dropping on our camp. It does no one any good to talk about what happened to her, so I prefer not to. Besides, the scary shit you're interested in didn't happen until 2009.

In 2009 I returned from my fourth deployment to the Middle East and although I was living on Fort Bragg, NC at the time, my family was still in Gary so I came home to see them.

The first night I was home, my brother and I sat on our front porch playing a marathon game of Monopoly and around 10 PM my brother called for a time out to fix himself something to eat. After about 30 minutes of waiting for him, I went in the house to use the bathroom and found him sound asleep on the couch. Instead of waking him up, I did something that to this day I can't explain; I jumped into my car and I drove out to the apartments where my ex-girlfriend and her friend were murdered.

The neighborhood had changed drastically since she lived there. Back then, it was perfectly safe to walk your dog at night, ride your bike around the block, or just sit on the front steps and tell ghost stories. I wouldn't recommend doing any of those things today, not even in the daytime.

It was so freaking weird pulling into the parking lot of her old apartment building after so many years and after what had happened there. I backed into a parking space, turned off my headlights and sat there quietly. I tried really hard to imagine her walking out of her apartment the way I'd seen her do hundreds of times before when we were kids; when she was alive. From where I was parked, I could see the blue light glow of the television sets inside of some apartments. I stared at my girlfriend's old bedroom window and wondered if the people inside had any idea of the horrible things that took place there.

It's funny how thoughts just pop into your head, and as I sat there, I remember wondering if Indiana had the law that required a seller to inform a potential buyer or renter of deaths that occurred on the property before they bought or rented it.

I also couldn't help but smile when I thought about the two of us at the Y & W Drive-in on Broadway. During the summer months, we went to the drive-in nearly every Friday and Saturday night.

I remembered the time she borrowed her mom's car to go to the drive-in, and the headlights stopped working. No matter what we did, we couldn't make the headlights come on, so we couldn't leave the drive-in.

We tried all night long to get a hold of her mom who was out with her boyfriend, her older sister who lived in Crown Point, and just about any friend we could think of, with zero luck. So, with no other options, we decided to wait until the very last movie ended and then make a try for her apartment, which was less than four miles away. It was a solid plan, we'd hit Broadway, turn right and at the next light by the Dairy Queen we'd turn right again; then another right on Harrison, and then a left turn here and a few more turns there and it was a straight shot to her apartment.

But just like in that song, "Wake up little Suzy," we both fell sound asleep. I remember someone who worked at the drive-in knocking at the car window asking if we were alright. We had no idea what time it was, but it was already getting light out.

We were so freaking scared. I remember that as we drove out of the Y & W over the bumpy gravel road, the headlights would come on and then go off again and by the time we turned onto Broadway, the headlights came on and stayed on.

When we got to her apartment, I climbed out of the car and started walking home. No sooner did the door shut behind her that I heard her mom screaming at the top of her lungs. Even more than half a block away I could still hear her mother raising hell. I also remember the nine mile walk back to Gary, in my platform shoes.

And then the wonderful memories were interrupted with the sick thought of her being mutilated less than 15 feet from where I was currently sitting. Did she scream as loud as her mom screamed the at her the time that we spent the night at the Y & W drive in? Could her screams be heard way over where I was when I heard her mother screaming at her?

From where I was parked, I could see that someone in her old bedroom was flipping through channels on their television. Below her old bedroom window, was the very door that the person who killed her walked through. I couldn't help but imagine the sick bastard walking through that door and up the stairs into the apartment where, according to the police, found my ex-girlfriend and her friend sleeping and killed them in the most disgusting unimaginable way possible. I know that she wasn't wearing anything by the time it was all over, but I've always wondered if she was wearing her favorite cookie monster PJ's when it started.

I had joined the military right after high school so I wasn't home when the murders took place. In fact, I didn't even learn about the murders until after I returned from an 18-month overseas tour.

My family still lives in Gary and in Merrillville so I come home at least once a year. But never before the night I'm I telling you about, had I ever once considered going anywhere near that place. I would often go out of my way to drive past the elementary school where she and I would meet on summer mornings and make out. I'd even make it a point of going to Shoop's where we'd go for those huge burgers; not the one in Crown Point but the one in Merrillville across the street from the big cemetery.

I'm a very nostalgic and sentimental guy, but no matter how sad I felt I could never cry when I thought about the murders. For many years I couldn't even bring myself to admit that it actually happened. Even after all of these years and as many times that I've read and re-read the newspaper accounts of what happened to them that night, I don't think I've fully accepted it.

OK, enough of the sentimental bullshit, let me get to the stuff that I think you're interested in.

Beginning the day after I sat outside of her old apartment, some seriously weird things began to happen. For example, the very next night, I hooked up with my best friend Eddie and with nothing better to do and nowhere to go, we drove around a bit and ended up at this place on Broadway in Merrillville. Keep in mind that no one, not even Eddie and I knew that we were going to this place.

We had been there for about an hour, drinking beer and catching up on things when an employee with a heavy accent, called out my first and last name and said that I had a call from; and then clearly said my dead ex-girlfriend's first and last name. That scared the life out of me. I didn't do or say anything, I just stared at the guy waiting for him to say something like, "Come on Dennis, it's just a joke."

Eddie wasn't scared, he was mad as hell. He marched over to the employee, grabbed the phone out of his hand and demanded to know who was on the phone. But as soon as he delivered a brilliantly crafted inquiry, the person on the other end hung up. I remember the employee telling Eddie, "You tell your friend to no call here again."

That scared me so bad that I couldn't even think straight. I was actually afraid to drive Eddie back to his house which was over by Riley Elementary School, not because of the neighborhood, but because I knew that after I dropped him off, I'd be by myself.

When we left the bar, I insisted that we go to the Star Dust bowling alley in Merrillville (now Hobart), because I needed to be around lights, people and noise. After a couple of hours of playing pool, I dropped him off at his house and went back to my parents' house without any further incidents. However, the next night things got worse.

The next night I was sitting in my parents' house watching TV, still very much shook-up about the night before, when a car pulled up directly across the street. I immediately turned off the television to kill any inside light (something you automatically learn to do when you grow up in Gary) and peaked through the blinds to see who was outside. I'm a classic car lover, so I immediately recognized the car as a 1964 Ford, Mustang.

Aside from the fact that a 1964 Mustang is cool as hell, there wasn't anything really significant to this one except for the fact that it was in need of some major body work. And then I got the creepiest feeling run down my body, beginning at my temples, down my spine, to my tail bone and then down both legs to my feet. As I was staring at the car, I suddenly remembered that I've only known two people in my entire life who owned a 1964 Mustang. The first, was a guy who used to be in love with my oldest sister when I was a little kid, and the other was Sandy (not her real name), the girl who was murdered alongside my ex-girlfriend.

Sandy was also the girl who talked my ex-girlfriend into breaking up with me right before I joined the Army and moved away. Although I only met Sandy once, I despised her instantly, probably because she didn't hide how much she instantly despised me.

Sandy was much older than my ex-girlfriend and also a nomad pothead who latched on to my ex-girlfriend because she needed a partner in crime and a place to stay. The fact that my girlfriend was under age when they met didn't bother her a bit. My ex was the perfect score, she was naïve and very pretty; two things that Sandy was not, and she practically had the apartment she and her mother shared to herself because her mom had pretty much moved it to her boyfriend over in Munster, Indiana.

I know just as sure as I know that you're sitting in front of me, that Sandy knew the bastard who did those unspeakable things to them. I have no doubt in my mind that she invited that bastard over to get high and that's why he was there.

I don't know where Sandy got the car from, I seriously doubt that she bought it because she had no source of income, not even enough to buy gas. What I do know is that she drove one and it was a piece of junk like the one parked outside of my parents' house that night.

I couldn't see who was in the car, but I wanted whoever it was in it, to know that I had eyes on them, so I turned on the porch lights. I kept hoping that a neighbor would come running out of their house and jump into the car and drive off in it. But that didn't happen. Nor did any other cars come up the street to shine their head-lights on it so I could see who was inside of it.

The car sat there for about twenty minutes then slowly pulled away. Once it was down the street, I pressed my face against the screened window and saw the car turn right and it was gone.

Creeped out yet? Hold on, it gets better. A few days later, while I'm still freaked out over the bar incident and the car outside of my parents' house, I was sitting in my parents' house watching re-runs of "Creature Features," hosted by a Chicago talk show host who went by the name of Svengoolie, when the phone rang. It was a little after one in the morning so I was expecting to hear one of my brothers or sisters on the other end asking if I wanted them to pick me up (I come from a family of night owls) and head over to Chicago. But instead, it was a young woman whimpering incoherently. In the back ground there were other voices which were not audible, but I could tell that whoever was in the background was arguing. One of the voices was very loud and aggressive but I still couldn't make out a single word they were saying. It was like listening to a conversation under water. As the people in the background got more and more agitated the girl on the phone stopped whimpering and began to scream really loud. I can only liken it to a child being tormented by a mean kid with a dead rat or something else they were terrified of. And then one of the voices in the background screamed "No!" and the connection ended.

The girl whimpering on the phone didn't sound like my ex-girlfriend, but then again, I had never heard what she sounded like while waiting her turn to be mutilated. Maybe the girl whimpering on the phone was her buddy Sandy and maybe it was my ex-girlfriend in the background begging for her life. Or maybe the whole thing was a sadistic joke.

Is this a ghost story or just a real nasty heartless joke? If it was just a cruel joke, all I can say is, "good job," because it scared the hell out of me. And if it's not, I really hope someone goes to that apartment and frees their spirits so they can finally rest in peace.

I've had four combat deployments since 2001, I've even been awarded the Bronze Star, and I am being one hundred percent sincere when I tell you that nothing, I have experienced in war has ever scared me, but this did.

Chapter Ten

Night of the walking dead chick.

The person telling this story is Eddie, and he currently works for US Steel and lives in the Gary neighborhood of Miller Beach.

It was a beautiful Midwestern summer night and my best friend Joe and I were sitting on the hood of my car outside of my brother's house in Merrillville, Indiana, while I babysat my nine-year-old nephew who was sound asleep inside of the house.

My car was parked at the end of my brother's long drive way with the front of the car facing the house and the back tires on the road; the car was actually blocking the sidewalk. Why we were parked that way I don't remember but I'm sure we had a good reason for it at the time.

So, there we were laying on the hood of my old clunker with our backs against the front windshield talking about cars, life after graduation, and of course, girls.

My brother's old house sat in a cul-de-sac adjacent some railroad tracks which have since been removed and converted into a walking path. As mentioned, the house had a long drive way that led to a detached garage that was practically behind the house.

The house also had a huge back yard and beyond that, there was probably 300 acres of woodlands, which ultimately ended up at the back fence of the Inns Brook Country Club and Golf Course. The entrance to the country club is on Taft Street.

If you walked out of my brother's back door and looked to your right, less than 20 yards away are some apartments where two young women were brutally murdered years earlier. From what I remember, the murderer tied the two young women by their necks to door knobs and then mutilated them with a broken bottle.

From where we were, directly behind us, right in the middle of the cul-de-sac was a small grass island with a tall street lamp in the center. To the right of us were three homes. At the end of the street, the sidewalk wrapped around to the left and lead directly to the front of those same apartments where the two women were murdered.

My head was turned to the right and I was looking at Joe when in the distance I saw a young woman walking up the sidewalk towards us. I remember asking "Joe, who the hell is that?" Although she was a good 40 yards away from us when I first spotted her, in the time it took me to ask that question, she less than 40 feet from us and closing in fast. I'm not kidding you; she was scary looking.

Joe and I are not small guys and being both from Gary, there was very little that existed in Merrillville, Indiana in the 1980s that could scare either of us. However, what we saw that night scared the living crap out of both of us.

I'd heard of the "fight or flight syndrome," but I never actually knew how it worked until that night. To this day, I'm proud of myself and of Joe, because neither of us froze.

I slid off of the car like Bo Duke while simultaneously pushing Joe off of the car and screaming, "Joe, get in the freaking car!"

Joe, being a native of Gary like myself didn't hesitate or ask any questions, he literally rolled off of the car and in a flash jumped through the window and into the passenger's seat. But before he could lock the door or roll up the window, the woman was in his window. I mean she was literally leaning into the car through his opened window, and just inches away from Joe's face. The "woman," was about 20 years old, with long brown straight hair, with skin so pale that she had to be wearing some sort of cream or makeup to make her look that way.

Even though it was at least 75 degrees out that night, she was wearing a waste length tan colored leather jacket with fur around the neck. I also remember that she wasn't carrying a purse or a bag.

Joe recoiled from her head being so close to his face. She didn't smile or excuse herself for making us soil our pants, she just stared past Joe and asked me, "Where is the Inns Brook Country Club?" Joe looked down the end of his nose at her and with his left hand pointed towards my brother's house and said "It's that way."

Before we could tell her that she couldn't get there by going straight ahead because of the large wooded area and the large pond that she might fall into, she began walking up my brother's drive way towards the garage and disappeared behind the house. I immediately started the car, turned on my high beams and floored it up the drive way to the front of the garage thinking that I'd see her walking into the woods. But just as fast as she appeared, she was gone. She disappeared so fast that we honestly believed that she must have walked into the back door of my brother's house.

Joe jump out of the car and ran to the back door of my brother's house and found it locked. Then we both sprinted to the front door and straight into my nephew's bedroom. Once we were sure that he was alright, we turned on every light in-side and out-side of the house and searched it, but we found nothing. We laugh about it now, but at the time, neither of us would go back outside to turn off my car; we were that freaking scared.

What made things even creeper, was that the apartment were the two women were murdered was visible from my nephew's bedroom window. From his bedroom window we could clearly see the front door of that apartment, which was illuminated 24 hours a day by a bright yellow light. And there was still crime scene tape across the apartment door, even though the killings had occurred more than a year earlier, the case hadn't been solved yet.

We never found out who the woman was or where she went. So was what Joe and I experienced that night and what happened to those women in that apartment connected? I haven't a clue. All I do know, is that it scared the heck out of us.

Chapter Eleven

The witch in our back yard.

The person telling this story is Jorge, a retired lab technician who still lives in the very house where this incident supposedly took place.

There was always something weird going on in our neighborhood, mostly because the majority of the residents were elderly first-generation Americans from places like Macedonia, the Ukraine, Russia, etc. and either didn't speak English, suffered from dementia, or both.

I have tons of wonderful memories from growing up in Glen Park back in the 1970s, but my most memorable one is also the weirdest.

My father was working the early morning shift at Inland Steel which meant that he would get up at 4 AM, have some coffee, and then head out the door. My mom would wake up with him to make his coffee and pack his food for the day.

One morning I was in my room secretly talking on the phone to a girl I had just met when the door to my bedroom slowly opened and my father firmly said, "I know you're not asleep, come out here right now." I had no idea what he wanted but I was certain that I was in trouble for something. I walked out of my room then down the hall and into the kitchen where I found my dad and my mom standing in the dark. They whispered to me to be quiet, then guided me towards our pantry which had a window that overlooked our backyard. I thought they were nuts, but when I looked out the window, I got the shock of my life. In the middle of my mother's vegetable garden was a very old white woman standing motionless and just staring at our back door. It scared the shit out of me.

But nothing scared my mom or dad. I'm freaking out, thinking that there's a witch in our back yard who is wondering how she is going to get into our house and kill us and my parents were expressing pity for her.

My father figured that she was just some poor senile neighbor who had no idea of where she was. That explanation might have been easy to believe in the light day but at 4 AM and in the dark she didn't look like some unfortunate soul, she looked like a menacing diabolical witch.

We watched her for a few minutes and then as if nothing weird at all was happening, my father announced that he'd better get going. So, he grabbed his thermos, kissed my mom goodbye, and began walking towards the front door. I was right on his heels all the way demanding to know, where in the hell did he think he was going. To which he laughed and said, "To work, where else would I be going at this hour?" I asked him if he had lost his mind, and then reminded him of the she-devil waiting outside to scratch him to death. I wanted him to call the police or at lease wait until the sun came up, but he just chuckled and made some comment about me watching too many scary movies and then walked out the front door.

Once you stepped out of our front door, there was a porch and some steps that led down to the sidewalk. Once at the bottom of the stairs you either went straight ahead to the street or you followed the sidewalk along the right side of our house and directly into our back yard which is where the garden was, which is where the witch was waiting. And you guessed it, that's exactly the route my old man took because that's also where our garage was, which is where his car was.

What in the world was wrong with that man? Hadn't he ever heard of the exorcist? My mother locked the front door behind him and the two of us hurried back to the pantry window. The lady was gone, but where did she go? Then we saw my father come into view and pass directly between the garden where the old witch had just been standing and the pantry window. He whispered loudly, "I'm fine, go to bed." But I wasn't going anywhere. We watched as he disappeared into the alley where I was sure the she-devil was waiting to get him. After all, she couldn't have gone too far in the short time it took my father to walk to the back yard.

So now my father is in the alley, out of our view because the garage is between us and him. I could hear him manually opening the big garage door and then I heard the car start and saw his back-up lights come on and then saw the car in the alley. "He made it," I'm saying to my mom, but wait, now he has to get back out of his car, and lower and lock the garage door then get back into the car, all of which would give the she devil all the time she needed to attack him. Thank GOD nothing happened to him. In fact, nothing ever happened any of us when we lived in that house.

The witch showed up so often that we'd sometimes have people spend the night just for a chance to see her for themselves. We never knew which days she would show up, but when she did it was always at the same time, right around four o'clock in the morning but only during the Spring and Summer months. And then one day she just stopped coming.

I often find myself thinking about her. She probably was just some old lady suffering from dementia, but I couldn't tell you that for certain. Was this paranormal? I don't know, but it scared us more than any of those phony ghost hunting shows you see on television ever did.

Conclusion

If you ask just about anyone who lived or worked in NW Indiana prior to the 1980s what things were like back in those days, they'll probably smile when they try to describe it, back before everything changed. Depending on who you ask, they'll probably blame the demise of the area on the violent crime that began to run rampant in the mid-1970s. And if you ask the question in certain circles, you'll probably hear it all blamed on the Blacks and Hispanics. But if you study the region, it's obvious that long before Blacks and Hispanics became the majority in the cities of Gary and East Chicago Harbor, violent crime, prostitution, and police and political corruption were an everyday way of life.

Even the quiet, laid back town of Crown Point, was the scene of some gruesome ax murders near the end of the 19th century and in the early 20th Century, cop killings at the hands of gun totting stick-up men occurred in the area way too often.

The region produced a lot of really tough people because they had to be tough to survive the sometimes-extreme weather conditions and the dangerous types of jobs they had and the hazardous working conditions.

They came from all over the United States as well as from around the world. They brought their own beliefs, languages and cultures with them, and way too often, their ways conflicted with their new neighbors' ways and you'd have episodes of heightened human emotions that led to violence and even murder.

Gary is best known for three things, steel mills, Michael Jackson and murder. Gary actually held the title of the murder capital of the U.S. in 2004 and 2005, for cities of its size. Ironically, and according to some guy I heard on the radio, Gary only lost this nefarious distinction when there simply wasn't anyone left to kill.

I have no idea if there is any truth behind the long-held beliefs that hauntings occur when and where people died suddenly or violently, or when an ancient Indian burial ground is disturbed, or when the deceased left behind unfinished business. But if any of that is true, perhaps it can help explain some of the stories I've just shared with you?

THE END

Made in the USA
Monee, IL
20 December 2021